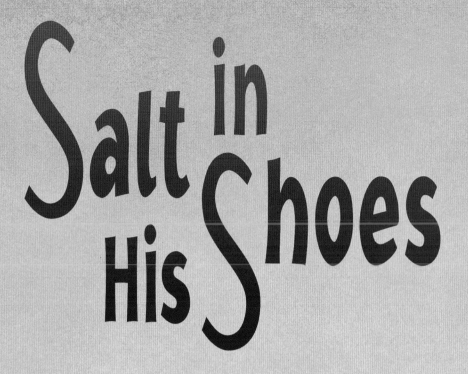

Salt in His Shoes

Michael Jordan
In Pursuit of a Dream

BY DELORIS JORDAN WITH ROSLYN M. JORDAN

ILLUSTRATED BY KADIR NELSON

SIMON & SCHUSTER BOOKS FOR YOUNG READERS

It is my hope that young readers and listeners will be motivated by this book to follow their dreams just as Michael followed his—by setting goals, working hard, and being dedicated. It's only when we do this that our dreams can and do come true. For that reason, I dedicate this book to the many children who are inclined to say "I can't," or "I wish I had talent," or "I wish I were gifted." To them I say, "You are gifted. You are talented and special. God has a plan for each of you; just believe in yourself and follow your dreams."

—D. J.

Every good and perfect gift comes from above. I give all praises to God for the gift to dream, the gift to believe, and the gift to be. I dedicate this book to all children who desire and are determined to mount up on wings as eagles and soar. By the grace of God you can fly. So just do it.

—R. M. J.

For Mom, Dad, Saliha, Amin, and Shedia

—K. N.

Acknowledgments

First, I thank my wonderful daughter and co-author, Roslyn, for her willingness to work with me, and for her inspiration and support. I am grateful for this opportunity to create with her—and grateful to her for showing her love, honesty, and courage.

Thanks also to Kevin Lewis, senior editor at Simon & Schuster Books for Young Readers for his commitment to this project and for making sure my voice was heard.

To Kadir Nelson for the imagination and great talent he brought to this project, thanks for the hard work.

To Amy Berkower, who worked with me to keep this project on time, thanks for the ideas and encouragement.

And finally to Michael, *Salt in His Shoes* is a tribute to him for not giving up, facing his challenges with confidence, and learning to never say "I can't." Thanks, son, for your support.

This book is also a tribute to Michael's siblings for the encouragement and support they have shown him along the way, as well as their continued efforts to fulfill their own goals.

SIMON & SCHUSTER BOOKS FOR YOUNG READERS

An imprint of Simon & Schuster Children's Publishing Division, 1230 Avenue of the Americas, New York, New York 10020. Text copyright © 2000 by Deloris Jordan with Roslyn M. Jordan. Illustrations copyright © 2000 Kadir Nelson. All rights reserved including the right of reproduction in whole or in part in any form. SIMON & SCHUSTER BOOKS FOR YOUNG READERS is a trademark of Simon & Schuster. Book designed by Paul Zakris. The text of this book is set in 14-point New Caledonia Semi Bold. The illustrations are rendered in oils. Manufactured in China.

24 26 28 30 29 27 25 23

Library of Congress Cataloging-in-Publication Data

Jordan, Deloris. Salt in his shoes / by Deloris Jordan with Roslyn Jordan; illustrated by Kadir Nelson. p. cm. Summary: Young Michael Jordan, who is smaller than the other players, learns that determination and hard work are more important than size when playing the game of basketball. ISBN 978-0-689-83371-7 1. Jordan, Michael, 1963– —Juvenile fiction. [1. Jordan, Michael, 1963– —Fiction. 2. Basketball—Fiction. 3. Size—Fiction.] I. Jordan, Deloris. II. Nelson, Kadir, ill. III. Title. PZ7.J76825Sal 2000 [E]—dc21 00-020539

0522 SCP

Michael loved to play basketball.

Every Saturday, he followed his older brothers, Larry and Ronnie, to the park, hoping that they would let him play. And if one of the guys who usually played with them didn't show, they always did. But there was one problem: his name was Mark, and he was the tallest boy on the court.

"What's the matter, Mikey, too short?" Mark flapped his arms in Michael's face.

"Over here!" shouted Larry. But when Michael threw the ball, Mark's long arms came out of nowhere and knocked the ball away. It flew into the hands of a player on Mark's team, he made the basket, and the game was over. Just like that.

"I am really sorry, guys. If I were taller that wouldn't have happened."

All the way home Michael apologized. Even though no one was mad at him.

His oldest brother, Ronnie, tried to cheer him up. "Look, little brother, you played good today. Don't worry. We'll win the next time."

When they got home, Michael went into the kitchen where Mama was cooking dinner. He was still disappointed, and she could tell.

"You guys lost again today, huh?"

Michael nodded.

He sat quietly for a minute, then said, "Mama, how can I grow taller?"

Now, Mama knew the answer to a lot of questions, but this was a tough one. She thought for a moment as she sprinkled salt and pepper on the chicken she was making for dinner. Then she smiled, looked at Michael, and said, "Salt."

"Salt?" Michael looked at his mama.

"Salt in your shoes. We'll put salt in your shoes and say a prayer every night. Before you know it, you'll be taller!" she replied.

"Salt in my shoes?" Michael said quietly to himself. Surely Mama was teasing. He sat staring out of the window trying to figure out how salt was going to help him grow.

He noticed the rose bushes outside in Mama's garden. They had grown
high along the fence, and roses of all colors were blooming on the vines. He
thought to himself, *I remember when Mama first planted those bushes.*
Michael's face lit up. *If Mama knows how to make those rose bushes grow
taller, then maybe she's right. Maybe salt in my shoes really will help me grow.*

Growing more excited, Michael twirled around and started asking lots of questions. "Mama, how long will it take? And how tall do you think I'll get?"

Smiling, Mama sat down next to him and explained. "In order for this to work, the most important things you have to do are be patient and listen to what I tell you, and say your prayers every night."

Listening carefully, Michael shook his head. "Okay, Mama, I'll be patient. But what does saying my prayers have to do with it?"

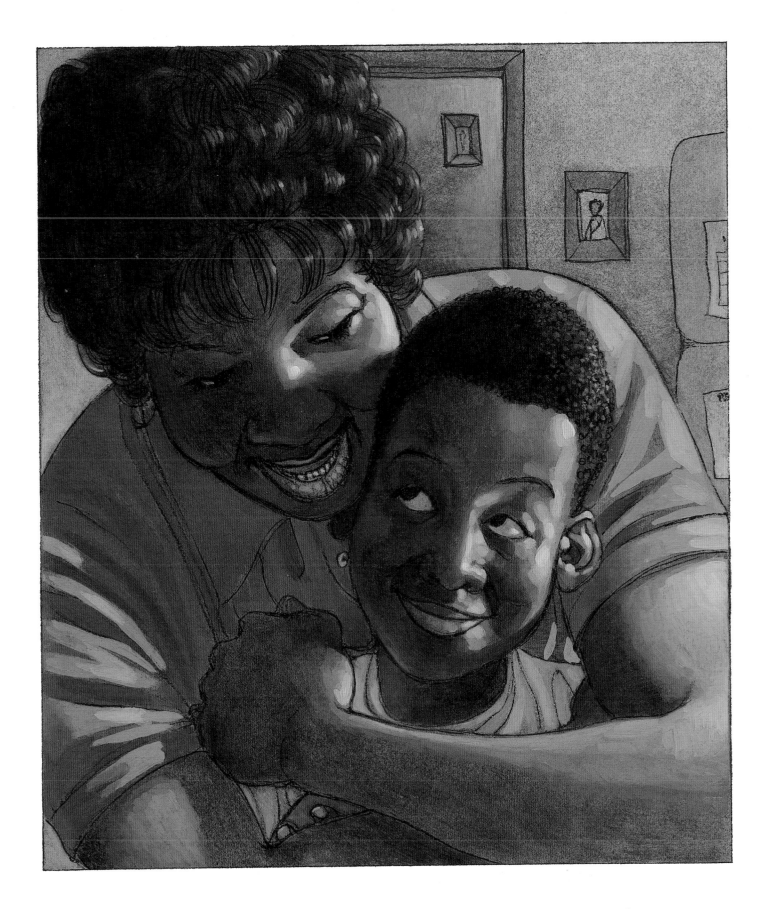

"Everything," Mama replied, and she hugged him. "Now go wash up and tell your brothers and sisters to get ready for dinner."

Michael dashed out of the kitchen, almost knocking over his father, who was walking in. "What's he up to now?" asked Daddy.

"Oh, the usual," laughed Mama, "chasing a dream."

Later during dinner, Mama noticed that Michael was barely eating anything. He was already daydreaming about being taller.

"Michael, first things first. You won't grow if you don't eat, especially your vegetables," Mama said.

"But I'm not really hungry," he said.

Raising her eyebrows, Mama gave him a stern look.

Slowly, Michael picked up his fork and began to eat. Minutes later his plate was clean and he was asking for more.

That evening at bedtime, Michael set his favorite game shoes on the floor next to the growth chart hanging on the wall. Then he put on his pajamas, said his prayers, and jumped into bed.

When Mama came in, Michael was fast asleep. By the look on his face she could tell he was already playing basketball in his dreams.

Standing by his bed, Mama sprinkled salt in his shoes. Then she prayed
quietly over him as she did all her children.

"Dear God, please help Michael to be the best he can be and to give
his best in all that he does. And Lord, could You please make him just a
little bit taller tomorrow than he is today? Thank You. Amen."

After that night Michael wore his favorite game shoes everywhere he went, even to church. And he stopped going to the park with his brothers on Saturdays. Instead he stayed home and practiced. He wanted to grow a few more inches before he went back to the park.

After two months of practicing and waiting patiently and praying, Michael stood next to the growth chart on his wall. Nothing. He hadn't grown an inch. He was disappointed, but he did not stop believing.

I've just got to give it time like Mama said, Michael thought to himself, and that's what he did.

Two more months of practicing went by and still nothing. Now Michael was becoming a little sad. Not only had he not grown one inch, but he also missed playing basketball with Larry and Ronnie. About the only thing he didn't miss was being picked on by Mark.

When the next Saturday came, his brothers tried to get Michael to go with them to the park, but he wouldn't budge. Mama had begun to worry. When she saw Michael sitting alone on the steps she said to Daddy, "Maybe you should go out and talk to him."

So Daddy went out and sat with Michael.

"What's wrong, son? You haven't gone to the park with your brothers for a while now. Are you okay?"

Michael didn't say anything at first. Then he looked at Daddy and said, "I thought I would at least be a few inches taller by now. I did everything Mama told me to do, but nothing's happened."

"Michael, why do you want to be taller?" Daddy asked.

"If I were taller I'd be a great player, and I could help our team win," Michael answered.

"But you *are* a great player, son. And you already have everything it takes to be a winner, right in here." Daddy tapped Michael on his chest. "Being taller may help you play a little better, but not as much as practice, determination, and giving your best will. Those are the things that make you a real winner."

Michael thought about what Daddy said for a minute. Then suddenly, he jumped up and took off.

"Where are you going?" Daddy yelled after him.

"I've got a game today, and I'm late," Michael yelled back.

When Michael reached the park the game had started. He sat on the bench hoping he would get a chance to play, and he did: The game was almost over and the score was tied when John, one of the guys on Michael's team, fell and hurt himself.

Here was Michael's chance.

Michael joined his team in the huddle as they gathered on the sideline for a time-out.

"Okay, the game is tied. All we need is one point. Who wants to take the shot?" Ronnie asked. He looked in Michael's direction. Feeling more confident than ever, Michael said, "I'll do it."

When the whistle blew and the game began again, Mark began to pick on Michael as usual.

"Still trying to play with the big boys, huh?" Mark taunted.

But Michael paid him no attention. Taller or not, he had been practicing, and today he was determined to win.

Larry threw the ball inbounds to Michael. Michael caught it, bounced it for a moment, and then took off running.

As he approached Mark, Michael shifted to his right. Mark
followed, but while he was still shifting, Michael spun
to his left. He stepped behind Mark and shot.
The ball arced far above his opponents'
hands and fell silently through the hoop.
Two points! The game was over. Michael's
team had won!

It was just as Michael had dreamed. When he realized what he had done, Michael took off running and didn't stop until he had reached home.

Bursting through the door, he shouted, "I did it, Daddy, I did it. I shot right over the tall guy's head and we won the game!"

Running in behind him, Ronnie and Larry joined the celebration. "That's right, little brother, you did it. You won the game for us."

Michael remembered the look that Ronnie gave him during the last time-out of the game and said, "No, *we* won the game, but I was the star."

They all laughed.

After that day, Mama stopped putting salt in Michael's shoes, but Michael did not stop being patient and working hard and praying.

So that must be what made Michael grow to be a six-foot-six-inch-tall basketball superstar.